The Color Blue of the Hermit's Robe

By Patsy Stanley

Copyright © 2020 to Patsy Stanley, author of this book. Use of any part of this book without permission from the author or her representatives or agents is prohibited by law. All Rights reserved. No part of this book may be reproduced, transferred, modified, or used in part in any way and in any form without the express written consent of the author, Patsy Stanley and her agents or representatives. This book is a work of fiction.

ISBN 978-1-7356266-4-2

LCCN 2020918028

Table of Contents

Part One	1
Part Two	20
Part Three	25
Part Four	32
Part Five	40
Part Six	45
Part Seven	49
Part Eight	55
Part Nine	60

Blue

Do the Universe a favor. Don't hide your magic.

Sometimes your sweetheart has to operate from the sidelines.

Goin' down to Nazareth
got a hole in my left shoe
faded out my clothes
from walkin' in
the mornin' dew

Part One

In my younger years, I fell asleep when my head hit the pillow. Or sleeping bag. Or rags piled up in a corner. Or the front seat of my latest old land yacht or RV.

I am an admitted hermit, a recluse, for I can't stand much of the world. Never could. Not one day of my life. I spent years on the road out of a deep need to stay away from folks. Well, some good luck is always better than none, and I was lucky.

I like to see the world, but not the people in it. I don't like most people. I never wanted to hermitize to one place's beauty and have that make me happy the rest of my life. But I did that, in the end.

When I was young, I wanted to shop around. Mainly 'cause I hadn't found my right place on this planet yet. My own Earth chakra. I knew I would know it when I got there. I hoped back then that I would find it in this lifetime.

I figured God might not have that planned for me, but I was sure gonna' try to find it on my own, no matter what God said. I was wrong. But that's the way I used to be...

I took after my parents. They were rovers, too, with the same inner constitutional needs driving them. They were not, and I am not very competent in big city ways. On a scale of one to ten, my outer world functioning level fluctuates daily because it is glued to my instinctive notions tighter than Velcro. I may be able to go out there, and maybe not. Now that may not sound like much of a problem, but my instincts change direction whenever they need to. The change is always on my behalf. I have lived my life trusting them completely in order to stay alive and safe. But sometimes the changes are sudden, and sometimes I don't know why.

But my mind is good, and my hand is good with a hammer and nails. No problems, there. Us three are all hard workers and use common sense. We just don't like much of what we see out in the world, so we move away from it.

Because of this condition, my parents and me, Jim and Dossie Griggs, and their son, that's me, Hector Griggs, spent our lives trying to keep away from others miseries. Mostly brought on by themselves. Keeping away took its toll, but got pretty easy after awhile. We need our vitality to live, so we quickly got good at avoiding people and their problems. Unless there was a reason to fool with them, we didn't. Simple as that.

Part of it was that we were backwoods people. Hidden children who were never trained to be social or in any way adept at "front porch" smiling and talking. We weren't told where the "back door" was either.

We were simple. Takes too much energy to fake it. We got better things to do. Like bein' real. We may be backwoods people, literally are, but we shine with our own kind of light and we know it. Like the good book says. And the Buddha.

My parents never asked me to call them mom and dad. Just Jim and Dossie.

They said that a' way, our karma wouldn't be so damaging to each other when they or me made a mistake. 'Cause all people make mistakes in life and pay prices. And that way, other folks wouldn't expect us to act like they did.

Grandpa and Grandma Griggs on Jim's side, and Grandpa and Grandma Disher on Dossie's side, were families too big and busy and mouthy mean for my parents to stand. There was plenty of incest and unrest on both sides of their families. Jim said the whole bunch was slicker than greased pigs and just about as loud and greedy.

It was our families that got to thinkin' that Jim and Dossie and me was demons because of our unusual beliefs, which did not fall in line with the hellfire and brimstone church they all attended sometimes.

Dossie said she was glad, and always would be, that she'd stayed with cousin Zelda Jean Franklin in Minneapolis for the summer when she was sixteen and got converted to a higher way of thinking. She learned all about Catholics and Buddhists and such from Zelda's free thinking family. She'd soaked up the books in their big library. She'd chosen the Buddhist path and came home to her family in the fall a changed young woman.

They didn't notice at the time, for she wasn't much of a talker with them.

She didn't care if her bunch went to church or not. Sometimes she went with them. They were never very steady churchgoers, just family members who came up with reasons to not show up on Sunday. They didn't want to part with a nickel on top of being told what to do. They always said they were off squirrel huntin', or they'd come down with somethin' contagious.

They usually overlooked Dossie, calling her odd. But when Dossie went to the woods and "Ohmmed," and talked about chakras too many times, they all began to pay attention.

Plus, she'd taken up with Jim Griggs, my father. They didn't mind him too much, but he wouldn't make Dossie mind. In fact, he let her have a mind of her own, and the upshot of that, was that he became a Buddhist, too.

They got engaged but never married. Everybody fixed up an engagement party and had a big time. They moved in together, and all the trouble died down for awhile. Then I come along, and it all stayed died down 'til I was four years old, old enough to start wearing something besides a night gown to sleep in at night.

That's the year Aunt "Lassie" Lassiter come to stay with the Griggs. Aunt Lassie moved from one relatives' house to another's house, until she wore her welcome out and moved on.

She was Grandma Griggs sister, and they were none too happy with each other. Aunt Lassie run through everybody in the bunch with her preachy ways until she got down to the bottom of the barrel. That meant us.

Jim and Dossie didn't want a turn with her, for she'd already spread it around that she was on a mission to make 'em marry. She was going to move in with us with a view towards eradicating Jim and Dossie's heathen beliefs and turning them back to the hellfire and brimstone church ways while upgrading the family with their marriage.

That's when we left. We'd had enough of a lot of things anyway, so it was a good, timely thing to do. Jim hotwired Grandpa Griggs old black coupe and we snuck off in it one night when they were all out hunting.

Jim left money for the coupe, so Grandpa Griggs wouldn't call the police on him.

I always liked an adventure, so I was just happy as a clam to get away from my bothersome cousins and the girls who held me down and measured my private parts, then let me go, laughing and waitin' for somethin', I never knew what.

We junk trailed it all the way over to Dewberry's Hill, where Jim stopped the car.

"Reckon it's time to git rid a' the rags."

I watched while he pulled the rags loose that was trailing the back of the car. He pulled them loose from their two short ropes, untied the ropes, and hid the whole mess in the woods. They'd drug along behind the car to keep anybody from tracing our tire tracks. He got back in the car.

"Time to move on."

We rode off into the night. I looked around. The dim light coming from the round dials on the dashboard up front looked cozy. Outside, it was black as pitch. The headlights give off a strong beam, like they knowed where they was a' goin'.

I dozed off. Woke up when I heard the car door slam. We was at a little ol' country store and gas station. It was just breaking dawn. Jim got out and strolled inside to pay the man for gas. The man come out to pump the gas. That's the way they did back in them days. Jim opened the hood to check the oil. He pulled out the dipstick, wiped it off, and studied it.

"How is it?" The gas station man asked.

"Don't need no oil yet," Jim answered him.

Yes, life was simpler back then. We were tin can tourists in America. All these years I've kept it simple by stayin' road ready. Keepin' good tires on my cars. Keepin' cars that run good. Lookin' up places to hide. My exit on wheels. Away from potential kids and wives and being stuck in one job in one place forever. I've loved a few and left 'em. They did the same to me too. You see, there's lady roamers, too. Not too many. Just a few. We run across each other in campgrounds, mostly.

After awhile, Jim and Dossie bought a pull trailer. That was better. A step at a time. Finally, they bought an RV. That's as close as they ever came to havin' a home.

We all knowed the ins and outs of campin' and what was needed. Learned all that by the time I was nine years old. Back then, I was already reading books.

Jim and Dossie made me learn to read and write and do arithmetic. They stopped at the thrift stores and got me books on ever' subject you could think of, mainly, whatever the store had to offer.

Now Jim, he worked at whatever trade he could find. He was a jack of all trades. Dossie worked in grocery stores stocking or cashiering, or as a janitor, whatever she could find. Neither one of them minded any kind of work. When we got a little money ahead, we moved on to greener pastures.

To make ends meet and save back a little extra, Jim played the guitar and Dossie sang hymns in the little churches we found along the way when we stayed any place for any length of time.

Jim and Dossie were devout about Jesus and Budda and the stars in the heavens, but not God and not Heaven itself. But they kept their mouths shut when they got singing jobs, and gratefully accepted any forthcoming donations.

Now, time went on and it come time for my tenth birthday. By then I knew the lay of the land backward and forward in some of the national parks and any place else that we stayed that was still wild and free. Not many humans in them places. Just a few hermits, like us.

Well, Jim and Dossie started a set of encyclopedias for me on my tenth birthday. I got volume one of my encyclopedia set and a cake and orange soda that day.

After that, we'd stop in a town for awhile, and they'd get a library card and borrow an encyclopedia just before we left town. Of course, the library people didn't know we were leaving town. We only did this in towns we wasn't going back to.

When my encyclopedia set was complete, they added great philosophers and famous people to my literary collection.

They stopped there because the books were startin' to take up too much space. So, I read them and kept a few and left the rest in picnic areas on tables and other wise places where people like me might find them. I inked out the library stamp in the front first.

That was my education. That and Dossie singing hymns. We stayed in towns and went to plays. We learned together and learned plenty for backwoods folks. Dossie found an old wind up record player at a Salvation Army and bought it and some records. We didn't know much about music. We'd always listened in on the radio back home, but that was it. Just country jokes and country folks singing.

But one of the 78 RPM records was labeled Porgy and Bess. We listened, learned, and stopped in more thrift stores and searched for music, books, and records to keep and pass on. We hit on a gold mine. Seems people didn't want the kind of music we were lookin' for. Well, it was a sketchy foray into music education, but it satisfied us to listen to Mario Lanza, Hank Williams, Handel's Messiah, and Mozart. Like Dossie always said, "There's more than one way to skin a cat." Ugly saying, but true.

Dossie read and kept journals. She pressed flowers and leaves and twigs and taped them into her journals. And herb pieces with wax paper over them. Feathers. Jim and me drew the line at animal fur or bones.

The years passed, and we stayed on the move. There were thousands of small towns back in those days, no big freeways, so we never ran out. Most people stayed close to home and didn't travel much, for there were just a few blacktopped roads and no four laners. Those words hadn't been coined in America yet.

I learned to drive and fell in love a couple times with girls in picnic areas or in RV camps. I was always relieved to move on, though. Don't know what that was about, didn't care. My inner self was taken care of by nature, not by long winded girls picking over my emotional innards.

Yes, I got hormonal when I was teenager but I run through the woods and lived out in the clean air. Jim taught me the hunting and knife skills his forefathers taught his family. I took to that kind of learning like a duck to water. Dossie taught me to cook game and to find clean water. I enjoyed learnin' all of it. I knew how to build a fire and save myself in a forest. I could live out my life in one if needed.

Smoky the Bear come along and he was my hero, so I decided to go to forestry college. Jim and Dossie dropped me off at school. They stayed close by, camping in RV parks until they knew ever vein of sand and dirt and grass and trees running through 'em.

It took that long for me to get two years of forestry training under my belt, so I could get paid to be a professional hermit and get a professional hermits job out in the woods. Jim and Dossie were proud of me. I got a job real quick and made good money, too. Bought us a second used RV and set it up for just me. Jim and Dossie and me got good tents and we put 'em up outside our RV's when we stopped in the RV parks. We caravanned together with bicycles on the back and tents inside.

It wasn't unheard of to run across people who lived the same way we did, for the Great Depression had made being a hobo respectable, so we made a few friends here and there.

I liked studying different animals and their habits. I studied every animal I could think of. Raccoons, possums, squirrels. I didn't like real bears. Never have. Never will. Just Smokey.

Don't like mountain lions, either. Too mean and dangerous. I studied them just enough to know what to do around them to keep myself safe. I always kept a pistol handy. Still do. Hid on me. I made me and Jim holsters out of soft deer leather to carry them in so nobody would notice. We carried them when we went into the woods. We were both handy with any kind of knife. So was Dossie. We did all right.

Anyways, I liked studying the animals. After squirrels, rabbits and pheasants, which we hunted to eat, I branched out into studying plovers. Which meant we needed to live near the ocean for awhile. We stayed there awhile, then it was back to the inland forests for us.

Next I started studying trees. I studied beech trees first. Their habits and where they grew. What kind of birds nested in them. What kind of soil they grew in. From there, I moved on to wondering about the Redwood forests in northern California.

Dossie and Jim and me went and camped in the Redwood forests and lived in pure awe the whole time. We stayed that way for two winters before we left. Wasn't no hunting there, and Dossie and Jim and me found short term jobs until our time run out.

Then I decided to study cacti. Which meant I needed to move to a desert. I moved to New Mexico because Arizona had too many people in it. Utah didn't appeal either. So I chose New Mexico. Jim and Dossie started traveling the back roads of Colorado and New Mexico so they'd still be close to me and visit once in awhile.

I found a little spot of desert that called to me not too far south of Albuquerque. One little town there. A shabby, little old town, with just a few people living there. Native Americans mostly, for there was a reservation nearby.

I drove all around it. I spread out and crisscrossed the area, stopping for the night in what felt like promising spots, like I always did. Jim and Dossie too. They told me what they thought of each place.

Finally, I found the right spot. It laid a few miles past a little white church. There was foothills nearby. Likely prospectors filled those foothills once upon a time searchin' for gold. Well, I was looking for the gold I needed. I didn't know what it was, but my instincts, honed by my natural livin', always told me what I needed to do next.

I pulled off the road and stopped. I got out and walked around awhile. So did Jim and Dossie. It didn't take long for me to know this was my place at least for awhile. I didn't like the heat or the dust or the lack of trees, so I knew I wouldn't stay here long. Just a little awhile.

What I did like was the vast, open space. It was a place big enough for some part of me that needed it. For awhile, at least. I wondered if that part was up for a permanent tan, because it was sure as hell going to be one hell of a task to stay here any length of time. Just to be in a big, empty space? Oh well.

I have always followed my Guides, Angels, and other good Beings all my life. They have protected me and kept me from harm and on the right path.

Jim and Dossie began introducing them to me when I was little and having one of my frequent bellyaches from eating anything I could get my hands on while their backs were turned. I wasn't hungry. They'd never let me go hungry. Some of the food we eat was questionable to other people, but I liked berries and leaves, and teas, and squirrel jerky. I just liked to taste everything back then. Had to, it seemed like.

We settled in and stayed a few days. I walked around. This was not a big empty space like it seemed. I knew about the Elemental kingdoms because of Dossie.

When I was little, she read C.S. Lewis and Tolkien to me. She told me that the Elementals lived in kingdoms. All the kingdoms were round and turnin' at different speeds. She said they were not spheres, but spheres were inside each of the kingdoms, like bubbles in a bubble bath, only more organized. She said plants, humans, animals, and everything else on Earth has an aura, a web around it to protect it and keep it alive.

Jim said we are part of a very organized higher spiritual system, one with a bunch of hierarchies inside of it. There were religious hierarchies in which people fought to the death over what the unseen results of life would be when we made transition. Each one had a different theory containing a different hierarchy and history. Though they arrived at the same place of not knowin' what took place after death, they fought and killed each other for the power and control religion held over people. Jim said the Golden Rule was the thing to go by. Do unto others as you'd have them do unto you. So we left it at that.

They both said everything is orderly and organized, even violence... but to avoid that whenever possible by readin' the signs leadin' up to it and exiting stage left, like any good actor would do before the fireworks started.

They said everyone was born either yang-violent natured, or peaceful-yin natured. That's because we live in a dual natured reality in which everything has somethin' called polarity.

I have seen things out of the corner of my eyes sometimes when I was young and out in nature, especially around flowers. Dossie said I was just seein' the fairies in flight.

This is what she taught me about fairies:

That fairies are energy beings akin to Angels. They are kept strong through our faith, our imagination, our loving, child-like belief in them. That's why they are here and sometimes we see them. Fairies are Elemental energy beings that work with the Elemental Kingdoms, and are most populous in the Air Element. They have the ability to manifest to us only at certain times because their strata is perpendicular, not vertical or horizontal, which gives them the powers of infusion, the ability to work with the life essence.

They are a part of the Hierarchies that govern the Plant Kingdoms. Fairies need no kind of government, except for supervision by the Rulers of their Kingdom. Fairies do not exist on the physical plane. They exist in a much higher vibration, or plane of energy. They exist in the fourth dimension and up. They are androgynous. But when they manifest themselves to us, it is as a male or female because that is the way we manifest. We assign them a polarity. They would manifest to us as however we looked. But their form is not like ours at all.

Fairies do not eat food. They obtain their sustenance from the fragrances of flowers, herbs, etc. The process they use is more than smell or taste. They bathe themselves in flower smells and it interpenetrates their bodies and reaches all parts of them. Fairies have no more internal structure than a wreath of mist, so they cannot be harmed or injured in the same way we can be. Heat and cold have no effect on them that is painful. Only density affects them. Fairies are entirely free from the curse of fear the human race carries. Fairies can only receive pain from inharmonious vibrations, and because they can move so rapidly, they can avoid and stay away from them. Fairies are the storytellers of the Plant Kingdoms. They have vivid imaginations. They can see the physical and astral planes of existence, therefore, they are able to build thought forms easily to tell their stories with. Fairies dislike and avoid human beings. We did too.

Now, Nature Spirits do not understand our language. They use telepathy. The sounds of our language are too dense and heavy for them and do not express life as they understand it. The sounds of our languages—all of them—are too low in vibration for them.

Nature Spirits sometimes (allow) come in contact with people who live solitary lives out in the country, or who spend a lot of time in Nature. People who are not in contact with other people very much have a much better chance of communicating with fairies and nature spirits.

This is because when a person has to mix with a lot of other people, their energy vibration is forced to lower, so they can get along with the other people.

Wind chimes

Flowers

Fairies love all forms of ballet. That music and its form is modeled on the fairies. Their favorite musical instrument is the flute. The music of flutes is used to relieve the passions.

In his youth, Krishna played the flute.

Later, I learned about blue fairies. I got pretty long winded with that, sorry, but that information forms the foundation for the end of our story, and why we did what we did.

Well, we settled into the desert for awhile. We found a little store not too far away. It was once a little church, but that didn't bother us none.

The folks there were like us, only they'd been settled in for awhile. Didn't ask why. Already knew. Dossie said that store was sitting smack dab in the middle of an energy vortex. A healing one. A good one. She said we didn't need an energy cleaning board for the groceries we bought there.

We stayed awhile and Dossie got to know the desert store owners. Dossie needed women to talk to, I guess. She spent plenty of time at the desert store.

Jim, Dossie, and me liked carnivals and went to them if there were any around where we were stayin'. We liked bein' in the smells and sounds and lights for a night or two. That's where I met Mona. Mona was not simple. She was one of the most complex beings I ever met. Emotional and bright, an Amazon, she tilted my world when I saw her at the carnival running the shootin' booth. I admired her bigness and her many tattoos of dragon flies. She revered dragon flies.

She quit the carnival and come to live with us for awhile. We went often into the desert and she would dance, surrounded by dragon flies. They loved her right back. She said after them, she might study dragons. She left when the call of the Wind got tangled in her hair and pulled her away from us. I let her go easy, for I understood very well the Wind's call. Once you learned its voice, it could only be obeyed.

I wasn't blue or anything like that after she left, but I did wonder sometimes how she was doin' and where she was at.

Jim and Dossie and me retained a calm surface in the face of any adversarial cruelty we run across. I learned to do it early on, and wore it like a good suit for the world to see.

Dossie was always calm. Calmness seeped into her being and smoothed out her internal path.

We were three world-mute, accepting, gentle people likin' what God give us to bear. Unless somebody crossed us. Really pushed us. Then we took care of business and got the hell away from them as soon as we could.

Well, that desert time passed, and we moved on. But I didn't forget Mona. Every time I saw a dragonfly, I said "hi" to her.

**Goin' out to find
a place where I can live fine
where I might comb my tangled hair
so the Master could
find me fair.**

Part Two

Well, we was travelin' again. Time went on and Dossie took to ailin' with somethin'. She wouldn't let us take her to a doctor. Her hair was growin' white. She growed a big belly and a double chin with plenty of hair on it. I thought about offerin' to cut it or braid it for her, so she would be neater lookin', but I knowed better than to offer.

We were also afraid to offer her the use of Jim or my razors. She ignored the hair and let it grow. A few wild hairs started growin' on her face, too. One was right above her eyebrow and she swatted it aside all the time. Kept sayin' she couldn't see good. Said it was her eyes but we knowed it was that hair.

One day while we was eatin', and she was swattin' away, I said, "Dossie, there's a bug or somethin' on your forehead."

I reached out real quick and ripped that wild hair above her eyebrow right out. I thowed it down and went back to eatin', calm as could be, like nothin' was going on.

She hollered real big and glared at me. I kept my eyes on my plate like Jim and I had planned the night before. Well, she stopped swattin' at her eye, which relieved Jim and my nerves a little bit.

But there was more things, too. She took up wandering through the woods huntin' up a creek to lay in every time we stopped somewhere. She needed the water, I guess. She'd jerk the door open and run into the woods like a deer that had been penned up, leavin' us to handle everything.

Yep. She quit pullin' her weight and didn't seem to give a damn any more.

She smelled different every day, too. Jim and me both knowed it. We knew better than to say anything to her about it. Jim got the worst of it for he was forced to sleep with her. I was real glad I had my own bunk in my own place.

Well, we made our circuit of the RV camps as usual, but Dossie didn't try to find jobs like Jim and I always did. She stayed home at our campsites and hunted up women to talk to who liked to tell everything they knowed and cry a lot. She listened to soap operas on the radio and wouldn't turn a hand. No more clean clothes, dishes, or home cooked meals.

We never quarreled at her. Not one time. Me and Jim picked up the slack at home. We strung the clothesline and washed the clothes in the creeks and hung them up while Dossie set in her lawn chair readin' True Love magazines. We hunted up mushrooms, berries, and greens. We knowed which flowers and roots to eat. We trapped rabbit and squirrel quiet like in the woods, brought the meat back skinned and washed and hid in a sack to cook and hunted deer in season away from other people.

We did it that way because most people liked the idea of going back to nature for a couple of days only. Their days didn't include huntin' or blue gill fishin'. They eat food they brought with them from home or bought at the closest grocery store.

We never bothered the weekend campers. We let them alone and they let us alone. We dried the deer meat and that took a couple of weeks, so we got a place quiet away from the parks in huntin' season.

No matter what Dossie did, she got no argument out of me or Jim. Somethin' was going on. We didn't know what the hell was wrong with Dossie, but we trusted that time would tell us what it was. Meanwhile, we kept our noses to the grindstone and our eyes on our plates. That means we worked hard, minded our own business, and let Dossie be.

Then Dossie took up followin' us into the woods, tryin' to save the animals from us. She cried if she saw a trap in our hand, so we had to stop trappin'. She started bringin' home animals and makin' pets of 'em. We left each place with more and more critters on board. When my place filled up with furry varmints, I called a halt to it.

"I'm turnin' them all loose," I told her in a firm voice.

"Me, too," Jim said.

We turned her varmints out into a nice woods and left with her hollerin' the whole way. Sometimes, a man's had enough and jist' can't take no more. It didn't do us any good though. Dossie jist' grabbed more animals and had the first bunch replaced in no time.

Me and Jim went off by ourselves to talk.

"What the hell are we gonna' do?"

Dossie had followed us without us a' knowin' it. We heard her voice from behind us.

"I know exactly what you're gonna' do. You boys are gonna' git' us a house. Somewhere out in the country. Some place where I can have all the pets I need without anybody else's say so on it."

We stared at her. She glared back at us, hands on her hips.

Jim said, "I don't want a house. I like travelin'. I like livin' on the road. You always did, too. What the hell's come over you, Dossie?"

"You heard me," she said and turned away, holdin' a little brown rabbit in her arms. We watched her waddle away.

"She's putting on weight again," Jim finally said to me. I took that to mean that she would gain until we got her the house she asked for.

"Well, we better plan on doin' it," I finally answered, thoughts of imprisonment in one place steady on my mind.

"Well, I guess we'll have to," Jim muttered. "Oh, hell...women!"

I stared at Jim. I'd never heard him say that before.

"I thought that a time or two about Mona before she left," I finally agreed.

"Well, that gives me some comfort," Jim said.

Goin' to see the Master
Gonna' catch that train if I can
Gonna' leave a trail behind
made of crumbs and tin cans

Part Three

We started havin' to look at life in a new way while Dossie fanned herself and thowed herself into every pond or water place we went by. We had to stop and let her take a soak over and over. We hoped the good thing we might get out of it was a change in her smell, but she still stayed the same. The damn critters loved it, though. They stayed snuggled up to her like she was their mama.

Jim prided himself on being able to change easy. He used to brag about it. But not anymore. Now, he just set thin-lipped and quiet and drove on and on, trying to figure out what the hell to do next.

Now, once a month we always stopped somewhere so Dossie could call the family back home for news. It wasn't time to do that, it was early, but Dossie wanted to call back home anyway.

Jim and me usually got to talk to somebody, but not this time. She let us know it was a private call. We went in the little store and moseyed around while she talked on the black dial phone hangin' on the wall in a back corner. We looked everything over. We were feeling pretty low, so we bought a Big Hunk candy bar, split it, and eat it.

Dossie hung up the phone and we left. She didn't tell us anything, but we wondered anyway. About three nights later she said we was goin' house huntin'. She said we had a purpose for being on the road now. We were to find her a house, and Grandpa Disher would pay for it. She said we needed to find somethin' quick before he died off.

Well, we didn't know what to do. Dossie was bossin' us around pretty hard. She was smarter than both of us in her woman's way, but we still needed the time it took to make such a big change.

We stopped at a place and stayed the better part of two weeks while Dossie read her magazines and didn't talk to us. She jist' set quiet and waited for us to get on with it.

Jim and me went off in the woods where we could talk without her hearin' us.

"Women are dangerous things," Jim said. I was forced to agree. I nodded my head.

"She's changed," Jim said mournfully. I nodded again.

"I don't think she's gonna' get any better. We're gonna' have to find her a place to roost for awhile. Find a doctor in the area to help her with whatever's ailin' her. When she gets better, we can sell up and move on again."

Jim looked at me, his Adams apple bobbin' hard. I could see he was caught up in strong feelin's right then.

I looked away and said, "Sounds like a plan to me. I'm in."

We walked back to camp. But we needed to wait until our innards settled down before we told Dossie. And we needed to set our minds to the new direction they would have to take.

Three days later, we told her at supper. The next mornin', we started our house huntin' journey. Now you might think it was easy, but it wasn't. There wasn't a thing about it that was easy. We had to stop in every town so Dossie could find out about any for sale properties located thereabouts. Then we had to go look 'em over. That took days. Every bit of it involved talkin' to a whole bunch of people we didn't want to. Dossie took over and did a lot of blabbin' like people do when they set on the front porch too long. Me and Jim shut up, ran errands, and waited it out.

Finally Dossie got real low about it.

"I don't know why I can't find the right place," she complained to us. "I've looked at everything I've heard about."

The animals snuggled around her churred and whined and cawed. We looked at her and sighed, deep inside sighs that could blow a man right off of a nearby cliff. We felt like we was standin' on the edge of one of 'em most of the time these days.

Jim picked up the black iron skillet and went outside. I followed him. It stunk in the RV. Jim hunkered down over the fire and set the skillet on the fire. He broke eggs into the skillet while I carved some dried venison into chips and tossed them in.

"I smell meat! Are you two cookin' animals again?" Dossie complained, standin' in the doorway of their camper. Me and Jim looked at each other. We were desperate men. Jim shoveled the biggest part of the eggs to one side for Dossie. Then he mixed the venison into the rest. Jim and me went into the woods for a walk after supper.

"It looks like we got one of them people who don't eat meat on our hands now."

Our lives changed. No more roamin' around, huntin' up little people, and learnin' their secrets or seeing Elemental farms or plantings out of the corners of our eyes. No more fascination with the mathematical intricacies of buttercups or daisies. Now we drove straight like arrows from town to town, trying to find a house for Dossie, who spent her time blabbin' and grinnin' at folks instead of stayin' out in Nature away from folks, where we belonged.

Dossie found places she went crazy over, but we couldn't stand them. They was all wrong for me and Jim. The houses were too big or two little or too old, and the land was wore out or barren. The barns didn't have good roofs or were too beat up with rotted wood. A good barn was a necessity to me and Jim. We didn't care much about the house. We'd leave that to Dossie and stay in our RV's. We didn't want one big barn. Just two smaller ones. One for Dossie's critters so we could stand to sleep in the house if we had to, and one for us to retreat to when necessary.

Well, time went on. It come into fall. We'd searched all spring and summer. Not a thing. We stopped at all vegetable stands now, so Dossie could stock up on food for herself and her critters. She'd made most of them into vegetable eaters, too, including Bob the bobcat, who howled real loud every time Jim and me cooked meat, though we tried to stay upwind from the RV. Dossie caught on to us and ordered us to move very far away from the RV to cook.

Well, in early fall we come upon a roadside pumpkin stand. We were on a gravel road out in the country, up near Wind Away Creek.

There was a mid size house with a big porch and a swing on it right behind the stand. There was a for sale sign in the yard as well as on the pumpkin stand. Three pumpkins were settin' on the stand. That was all. No other vegetables. Dossie studied the three pumpkins awhile and then said it was a sign. The sign of three. There was three of us. No other vegetables. So this must be the house we was lookin' for. She wanted all three of the pumpkins and the house too right then without even lookin' at it.

We knowed she'd been lookin' for a sign. That's how Dossie was. But Jim and me had been learning some hard lessons over the past few months. We had become cautious. Dossie hated caution these days. She considered it an enemy. She used to like it. She used to find signs and study things out for us. Not anymore. We were on our own now.

She stood by the pumpkin stand with her arms crossed. She was wearing one of Jim's shirts again. It struck her jist' below her knees. Jim was noticeably bigger than her, and she'd took up wearin' his shirts. He was down to three nowadays.

Well, desperate times call for desperate measures, so we roused the old folks dozin' on the porch with a view towards pumpkin buyin' and lookin' the house over.

They wanted the house gone quick, so they could move in with their son, who they said had plenty of room and was livin' by hisself', now that his unfaithful wife had run away. Well, me and Jim didn't want to know any more about that old story, so we just closed their voices out and nodded a lot. Me and Jim left them to Dossie's blabbermouth while we focused on the house.

It was a small farm. It set on ten acres. There were two smaller barns, a tractor, and fields to plow. We took the house. Me and Jim agreed, mostly because there was soft blue mountains settin' on three sides of it and a good, thick woods to hide in back of the place.

We drove Dossie to town so she could call Grandpa Disher. He wired the money for the place to the little bank in Wind Away Creek. That's where we settled down. For awhile, anyways. Grandpa Disher passed away before the next month was out. He passed away while we was still settlin' in. Dossie knew ahead of time because she looked up and saw a white hawk flying high and hollerin' down at her.

"Hollered at me jist' like Grandpa Disher allus' did," she informed us. "I bet he's passed on to a better world. Take me to town, so I can call home and find out what he's done now."

Dossie didn't drive. Didn't want to learn, either. We took her to town and she called back home. Sure enough, Grandpa Disher had passed away. Everybody back there got on the phone. They was mad at her 'cause all his money was gone. He'd sent it to Dossie, and they wanted it back. She hung up on them.

"I guess I won't be callin' back there no more!" she said, miffed.

**Don't need more strife
I'm a leavin' with my life
puttin' on my shoes
an' closin' the door**

Part Four

A new chapter began in our lives. We parked the RVs and set them up as usual. The house was empty. It needed cleanin', so me and Jim went at it, with Dossie workin' alongside, bossin' us and scoldin' us when we made her critters go outside.

But us two men were starting to draw new lines. And we meant it. We drew the line at poop in the house. From critters or people. There was a nice outhouse out back for people. Her chickens and the other animals could stay outside now. Dossie made us build fancy pens for her critters. Pens with doors and roofs. And big. She wanted porches too, but we wouldn't do it.

We worked and stood it until we had to get away from Dossie's house. We told her winter was comin' soon, and the leftover money from grandpa Disher was runnin' low. In desperation, we went into town, looking for jobs. I got one dishwashin' in the back of the only restaurant in Wind Away Creek.

I lived in hell the whole time I worked there, not because of the work, that was easy, but because of the cheerful, loud voices that kept changin' and a' comin' and goin', never endin'.

I quit after two weeks and went up one of the trails in back of the house for a few days. I camped out and trapped rabbit and squirrel to eat. When I was steady again with food and thought, I come back down to the house.

Jim was luckier than me. He got a job puttin' up hay for a farmer. *At least he gets to stay outside and away from people*, I thought resentfully.

Both our jobs would end soon and we'd have to find other jobs. We would both have to find long term jobs. A job filled with expectations that must be met if we were to keep it. We'd have to smile and lie. We'd have to kiss ass or brown nose to a degree, we didn't know to what degree yet, but it certainly would happen. All kinds of things we didn't have to do when we traveled.

When folks hired us and we told them we lived in RVs and moved around a lot, they took a nice tack with us. They knew without it being said that we didn't give a damn about their little social circle or who the big fish was in their little pond. So, they left us alone and we worked for them and then moved on. We didn't have to make friends or smile at their bullshit.

Well, we were in deep shit now! And it was all because of Dossie. Her fault. Every bit of it. Her cookin' was deteriorated to the point that me and Jim did all the cookin'. She run to the little creek on the edge of the property, took her clothes off, and thowed herself in it without checkin' for snakes or anything else first. Thank the lord for the good, deep well on the place, for Dossie used water like crazy.

Well, I got a full-time job at the feed store. Jim got a full time job at the lumber company. In our heads, we each told ourselves it was only a temporary job. That's how we was able to deal with bein' around people all day long instead of runnin' away. Two weeks at a time. All through the long-assed winter.

I walked by two houses to get to the feed store every day that winter. Spring come, and Dossie seemed to be feelin' a little better. We'd done our best all winter to get her to go to the doctor, but she wouldn't do it. Well, her belly went down a little, so we left her alone.

I walked by one of two out of the way houses, walkin' easy, likin' the warm spring air. Birds was out again, singin' and buildin' nests. All was well. I looked at the tattered fence I was passin' by. Then my eyes lit on the yard. It was a mess.

A woman about my age, thirties or so, stood there. She was wearin' some sort of tent thing, like Dossie would admire. Her hair was brown and red mixed. It hung long and loose. There was a wave to it, and a shine. I shuddered. I didn't want anything to do with women lately. Dossie had ruined that idea for me.

The woman ignored me. She was frownin' down at the new dug earth at her feet. I took off almost at a run.

But I'd already noticed her mistakes. The hoe was standin' wrong. The flower seeds was the wrong kind for where she was standin'. Them seeds called for full sun and no shade if they were to thrive. I couldn't get it off my mind, I mean the seed placement, not her. So, at noon one day, I purchased the proper seeds for the dappled shade around the trellis the woman had stood in. I walked by her place with the seeds in my pocket. Nobody was around, so I snuck inside and planted the seeds and placed everything where it should be so she'd know.

I didn't like to go straight home to Dossie and Jim, where I was no help, jist' a third wheel. So, I started tarryin' a bit on my way home and fixin' up the woman's yard. It was easy. I didn't fear getting' caught.

I'd already hid and watched, and now I knowed she went off to work somewhere ever' mornin' at eight and she got home at five thirty. Five days a week. That took up some of my time durin' the week after work.

I went up the trails in the woods and camped on the weekends. Eat meat and studied nature. Then I come back down Sunday night, took a bath, and went to work at the feed store Monday mornin' at six o'clock. I got off at three o'clock, so I had just enough time to keep the woman's yard up before she got home.

Her potted plants looked awful. Like the kiss of death had touched them. So, I trimmed, fertilized, watered, and replanted them.

One day I found a note with a muffin sitting on it. Blueberry. My favorite. I picked up the note and studied it. It said, "Thank you to whoever is saving my yard and plants from me."

I ate the muffin. It was a good one. I favored sweets anyways and had gone without a lot since Dossie stopped cookin'. I took the stubby pencil I carried in my pocket out and wrote on the note.

"Plant perincosis sibuls here. The little yellow striped bonnet flowers."

The next day I got another note. It said, "You do it. I'll kill them."

There was two blueberry muffins on a small plate on top of the note. Well, I planted them and eat the two muffins, but that was enough for me. I stayed away from her place for a week.

After that, I walked by and kept tabs. I looked straight ahead, so if anyone was there, they wouldn't see me bein' interested in her place.

Anyways, after awhile, I started taking care of the house next door to hers, too. I had to, because the old woman that lived there caught me tendin' to the woman's yard.

"So, you're the mystery gardener," she said, looking me up and down with squinty eyes.

"Well, I don't want her to find out," I answered steady like. My hands were full of plants. I set them down.

"Don't want no trouble. Don't want to git' to know anybody. Just like plants, that's all."

The old woman looked at me shrewdly.

"Well, I wasn't born yesterday. You're one of those Elemental men who are Pagans in their souls, aren't you?'

"You called me out right on that," I answered, though I didn't know for sure. Her look caused me to spill my guts.

"I like to travel. I don't like to stay one place very long. Don't like people enough to do that. Me and Jim are stuck here because of Dossie, my mother. Jim's my father. She's a...little under the weather—she's turned strange on us. Me and Jim, I mean. She bought the old Hodson place."

The old woman though about what I'd said for awhile. Then she said, "Well, I'll tell you what you have to do to get her well."

I waited.

"First, start making homes for the fairies and elves. Then blend flowers in here and there around their dells. Then when you find a pair, jist' leave them to themselves."

She grinned a long toothed smile at me.

I studied her and finally nodded. A poem. A mystery.

"Well, that's good."

I finished plantin' while she watched me. When I was done, I went home and never give it no more mind for Dossie was chantin' stuff and carryin' on from one of her books, and I'd had enough for the day. I went to bed early and slept like a log.

The next evenin', I went by the two houses on my way home, neither lookin' left nor right. At the end of the second house, I heard the old woman call out.

"Hey, come back here a minute. I need your help with somethin."

I didn't want to, but I turned and trudged back the way I'd come. I sighed. I might be in big trouble here. I would make sure my RV was road ready tonight, that's for damn sure. I might just pull out in the mornin'...

The old woman interrupted my thoughts.

She whispered loud.

"They've been waitin' on you all day. Get 'em to their rightful homes quick, okay?"

She grabbed up a basket and shoved it into my hands.

I took it and looked inside.

My world whirled in and spun. Then it stopped. I grinned. A real grin. Not the fake one I used for my boss. And other people. Then I laughed. The old woman did a little dance.

"Hurry!" she whispered. "She'll be home soon."

I stepped over the short white picket fence next door and got busy. They danced around and hummed soft while I put them in place. They soft-said their names and ages and the places they'd lived.

When I was done, I bowed to all of them. The fairies and elves and little people and the others whose names I did not know. Then I stepped back over the picket fence and handed the old woman the empty basket. She took it and shaded her eyes and grinned up at me. I looked into her old, wise eyes. I'd just been assured that there was magic in the world again. I'd almost lost my faith in it after Dossie went nuts on us. But it was back now.

"Prices have to be paid," she said.

I nodded warily.

"I'll come and see your mother soon."

I stared at her.

"I got a funny feelin' about that," I said and walked away.

I heard her laughin' behind me.

**Read a book awhile ago
that told me more
than I needed to know
'bout the ebb and flow**

Part Five

Dossie was wailin' again. She didn't know why. Or care. She kept on, windin' down in between to sniffles. Nobody to talk to. That's what it was. No women. Tears filled her already red eyes once again.

Jim stood up, a careful, blank look on his face.

"I'm gonna' check on a few things before night falls."

He was out the door in a flash. Dossie glared after him resentfully.

"Men! Worthless bunch when it comes to women's feelin's! Big louts!" she kept on goin'. I got up and walked out, too.

The old woman come to visit Dossie on Friday night. I'd already told Jim about her. We never kept secrets from each other. We stood in the yard and watched her knock on the door and then go in the house.

Before the old woman closed the door behind her, she give me and Jim a look that said stay away. But I snuck up on the porch and opened the door a crack to see what was goin' on and if we needed to protect Dossie from somethin'. The old woman was settin' on the couch holding Dossie in her arms like she was a baby. A big fat overgrown cryin' blabbermouth baby.

"There, there." I heard the old woman say to Dossie. "It's not as bad as all that. I know what's the matter, and so do you. I know what to do for the Change. That's what you're in. All women go through it. Your hormones are dwindlin' away. No more periods. No more bleeds. You are one of the ones who will be allowed become a Wise woman as your Change takes place. Not all are called for they have not earned the right. So suck it up."

The old woman glanced at the door. "Shut the door, boy," she ordered. "This is not for your ears. Go tell your father what you have heard, and stay away."

I shut the door and went to find Jim. He was settin' on a bale of hay out in our barn. I told him what the old woman said. That Dossie was goin' through something all women around her age went through. Somethin' called the Change. Jim studied on what I said for awhile.

Then he said, "I remember Ma a' havin' that kind of stuff go on, too. I'd forgot. Lordy!" he said, shaking his head. "Ma got crazy for awhile. But then she got better... "

He thought some more, then he said, "Oh man! I think we're in for it! As I recollect, it took Ma years to get it done."

"How many years?" I asked.

"Maybe eight or ten years."

We both stared out the barn door longingly at the road leading away from the house.

I saw the old woman a few days later. I asked her what she thought of Dossie.

"You're a man, so never you mind. I'm helpin' her take care of it."

"What do I call you?" I asked her.

"Grandmaw. You need one."

The next night, Dossie handed us a basket to take to Grandmaw.

"Be right smart about it," she said. "I don't want the ham or cornbread to git' cold."

We knocked on her door after I showed Jim which one it was. He handed her the basket when she answered the door.

"Buttered honey cornbread and a hunk of ham in here from Dossie, Grandmaw."

She frowned at us. We turned and left, the smiles wiped off our faces.

I went to the library to look for books explainin' the Change, but couldn't find any. I asked the librarian and she got all embarrassed and huffy with me, so I left. Don't plan on goin' back there again.

I got my nerve up and asked Grandmaw about it again one day after work. She said what

Dossie was going through was called menopause and most people never talked about it. We set down, and she enlightened me on that subject for awhile.

I went home full of news. I thought all men knowed somethin' about the deepness of life. I just thought that some of them took it wrong or was scared of it. But Grandmaw said only a few men was able to understand it. And I was one of them that might catch on, but only if I worked at it. She told me she knew about me and the fairies, and it was time for me to study Nature again.

I told her I had to have a job.

I was left to figure that one out.

She said the more I learned about women, the more I'd understand about Nature and the Elements. How all things work together. "There is a season," she said, "for all things. Everything has hormones and women who bear the children, have a different set than men. Men's hormones were blasty and straight. Women's hormones were circular and nesting."

She said to tell Jim. Now, how was I supposed to do that?

"Why don't you tell him?" I asked.

She said he wasn't the same kind of man I was. She said he was a man who stood in the middle of the worlds. He would listen to other men. What a burden to place on me when I was already knee deep in confusion! That was on

Friday afternoon. I didn't tell Jim anything. I went up the trails that night and didn't come down until Sunday, late afternoon. I was hopin' to avoid everybody, but Jim was waitin' in the barn. He was sitting on a bale of hay, listenin' to Dossie wailin' up in the house.

"I don't know how much more of this I can stand," he said.

I set down and said, "Well, there's more."

Then I told him what the Grandmaw said. I plumped it up a bit for he looked pretty hang dog.

"It git's over with, and she'll go back to bein' herself again," I said.

That was likely a bald faced lie if it was ever told. But Jim needed to have some hope. We listened to Dossie still wailin' in the house. Her critters moaned and groaned and yelped right along with her. We slept in the barn that night.

**Ain't seen a' easy Sunday
in a month or two
wonder where ever'body's
took their selves off to.**

Part Six

Now that we knowed what was wrong, we needed to figure out what to do next. The Grandmaw knowed plenty, but she'd give us too much to think about all at once. She said she was plannin' to come on Friday night to see Dossie again.

Friday night come around. I heard Grandmaw's knock at the door. I jumped up from the kitchen table where Dossie was eyein' the food Jim cooked.

Me and Jim headed out the door and for the hills by way of the barn. Up the trail we went. We went off on a tangent so nobody could track us. Dossie was on her own. Her and the old lady. They'd have to take care of their business themselves. We didn't want any part of it. They'd have to see to the critters for a change. Bet that would slow them two down an inch or two.

Well, we hunted and trapped and skinned the game out in a little clean creek up on the mountain. We buried the entrails and fur deep, so nothin' would dig it up. We cooked and eat all we could, then we packed the rest in our game bags and went down the mountain late Sunday afternoon. The meat would come in handy since Dossie, who could cook game better than anybody in this world, had become a vegetable eater.

We went down the trail and back to the house. Things were quiet, for once. Dossie was sitting in a rocker on the front porch. She looked peaceful and calm. And kind of fat faced. She noticed our glances and said, "It's Grandmaw's remedies makin' my face look that a' way."

We shrugged. Dossie had caught our thoughts before. It wasn't new.

She stood up. "Let's go inside," she said. We followed her through the door. Instead of the big mess she left the place in nowadays, it was clean. There was a fire in the little black standin' stove.

"Lookie here," she said. She opened the bedroom doors. Clean.

"Grandmaw Rose Butler's two friends come visitin' after youn's went up the trail and left me to do everything for myself. They come Saturday mornin' and cleared me out of my old space. They wondered why you two wasn't a' keepin' this place cleaned up."

She changed the subject.

"I want you two to go up the trails and search out these plants and herbs for me and bring em' back. There's instructions on here about how to gather them and what part."

She handed us a paper.

"Why, I don't even know what some of these plants are," Jim said. "I can't gather somethin' I don't even know the look of."

He looked at me. I nodded.

Dossie put her hands on her hips.

"Go to the library. Or better yet, ask Grandmaw."

We shuddered and turned away. We was already eatin' out in the barn and spendin' weekends up on the trails when we wasn't at work.

Winter was coming soon...

Dossie interrupted our thoughts. "Gather em' quick a'fore winter sets in," she prompted. We slid out the door.

Well, I knowed pretty good about these matters because I'd studied them in the Woodson Turner School of Forestry located up in the dells of Wisconsin. I soothed Jim.

"I'll look to it. You're her man, and I don't want you runnin' away."

It was supposed to be a joke, but he looked at me like he jist' might do it. Run away. I could see the thought had crossed his mind before. I was kind of dumbfounded.

Jim grinned at me. "Thanks. I don't mind tellin' you I'm as blue as can be over this whole thing."

I nodded. "Me too!"

We stared at the closed front door of the house. We could hear Dossie in there haranguing something behind it, maybe the kitchen sink this time. We heard her use a couple a' swear words.

"That old woman's learned her that language." Jim said. "She's made me move into the spare room in the back to sleep. She won't sleep with me."

I studied the ground. "Maybe that's best," I said. I grinned at him and pinched my nostrils together like something stunk. He blinked at me.

"Yep. No quarrel there. You smell better than she does these days. Not much though."

I nodded. We both turned and headed for the barn.

Goin' up the mountain
Gonna' gather bones and claws
Come back home
Put em' in jars
Save em' for the Master

Part Seven

Yep. The old lady that made us call her Grandmaw scared the hell out of me and Jim. And now she'd brought other women in that we knew brooked no pardon, to take up with Dossie. Two of them. We were outnumbered. Livin' in the barn and waitin' on the ladies looked like it was going to be a permanent occupation from now on.

Jim and me was overloaded. We stayed away from the house. We took up new habits. We dropped groceries off on the front porch, knocked, and took off. Disappeared. Dossie got happier but bossier. We heard her grumblin' and whinin' about us.

"Where the hell are those two men when you need 'em? You'd think they'd do better than to leave a sick woman all alone and on her own."

Dossie was plumb full of it these days. She couldn't see what was real if it was to come down the mountain and look her square in the face. She'd probably put it to doin' somethin' for her, too. Well, she had those three women backin' her up now.

We stopped payin' attention to her survival mode and waitin' hand and foot on her. We went into our own personal survival modes. Yep. Dossie had forced us into our own survival mode. Backed us into a corner with her ways. Full tilt. We snuck our things out of the house and out to the barn when Dossie was off on her daily short trips to nowhere.

It was touch and go, cause one of us had to follow her to keep an eye on her, so she didn't try to bring home another dangerous animal. She got lost a time or two, but we found her easy for we was good trackers.

One watched out for her while the other one sneaked into the house and grabbed a load of our stuff and run with it to the barn and hid it. A few trips was all it took us to move out of Dossie's house completely. And we was glad to do it. We made our beds in the barn and that was the way it stayed for awhile.

I still walked by the two houses—Grandmaw's and the other woman's—on my way to work. After I put the fairies and little people in the woman's yard to live, she put up a sign. It read "There is magic everywhere."

She left muffins or pies out ever' couple days. I carried them home so Jim and me would have a good dessert. I still took care of her yard.

I didn't need to meet another woman at this time. We had all we could handle back at the house with Dossie, her two new friends, Belle and Jincy, and Grandmaw. Yeah. We knew their names now.

Dossie had turned her life into a woman's world only. Men were to be their servants. But we were a wily twosome, me and Jim. It didn't take us long to figure out when the women would try to hunt us down and order us to do somethin' for 'em.

You see, women have very set patterns, even though they believe they don't. We drew our lines.

We brought home the groceries, set 'em on the porch, knocked, and took off. We had all our things out of the house now. Our belongings were in the barn and in our RVs. We washed our clothes in the creek on the edge of Dossie's property, hunted meat, and eventually, moved back into our RVs.

We kept our RVs shipshape and left the house to Dossie and her new sidekicks.

We was okay with it. Me and Jim acted like we didn't hear the women when they tried to boss us around. We did take their lists of herbs and plants and hunted them up on the trails on weekends because we were both interested in learnin' about the plants.

We peeked in the windows of the house one day when Dossie and the women were in the woods. They went with her now, so we didn't have to follow her. We first looked in the windows, then we opened the front door and slipped in. There was bunches of herbs hanging from the ceiling everywhere. Me and Jim's eyes started waterin', and we had to catch our breath. Back out the door we went.

"Lord have mercy!" Jim said.

Dossie put us to huntin' up mushrooms and other forest edibles. Then rocks. She ordered certain sizes and shapes. Then she wanted string and ribbons. Okay. We did it. We didn't want her puttin' a spell or something on us even though we didn't believe much in spells. It was just me and Jim now.

Well, the time come when we'd finally took enough off of Dossie and her bunch of women. Me and Jim was desperate men livin' in our RVs and staying away from the women. We started ignorin' 'em and stopped doin' what they said. We brought home groceries on Friday night which was payday. We bought and paid for jist' enough for Dossie and stood them on the front porch against the door. We quit knockin' and started amblin' away, takin' back our dignity.

We fed the critters and treated them right, but we turned the new ones the women trapped back into mountains. We sneaked the cats into town and turned 'em loose. More than two dogs was a misery. So was one. So we took them to a man livin' up in the mountains and give 'em to him.

Dossie and the women raised hell but we stood our ground. We wasn't gonna' leave Dossie like the women wanted us to. She was ours. Stinky and mouthy and fat and bossin' the world around. But still, ours. We wasn't going to put up with a bunch of critters that stunk and wailed and barked and grunted, though. Dossie filled that bill all by herself.

We had to buy the feed for their animals. The women knew we wouldn't let 'em go hungry. They had us pegged in some ways, but not in others. Things were perkin' along.

When I went to work, I started taking a detour so I wouldn't be goin' by the pretty lady's house or that old Grandmaw's house anymore. It was none of their business where I was. I didn't need any more trouble than I already had. Life was becomin' a worrisome thing.

We left that bunch to tend to the animals on weekends because me and Jim headed up the trails. Jim left her a note sayin' we was doin' other things in town and couldn't feed the animals any more at night either. That meant her and the women were forced to feed them daily, not jist' on weekends.

Dossie found out quick that she and that bunch of women would have to take care of any animals around the place. We hoped it would put her to thinkin' twice about takin' any more notions about gatherin' more animals on the place.

That lighnin' rod
sunk deep in the ground
gonna' take too many days
'fore that time slips back around

Part Eight

The war between me and Jim and Dossie kept on goin', but I saw that Dossie was startin' to miss Jim just a little bit. She started comin' out on her porch and starin' at the RVs—without her women. Jim said that meant she might be missin' him. Maybe me too.

For the first time, me and Jim headed out in my RV the next weekend instead of going up the trails. We didn't tell Dossie we was goin'. She was still bossin' the world around, and her cussin' had grown very explicit. And we was the main target. We needed relief. Well, we went to a nice RV park and had a good time.

When we pulled back in late Sunday evenin', Dossie was sitting on the porch in her rockin' chair. The other women wasn't around. She scowled at us and jumped up and went back in the house. Slam! Went the front door. We could hear pots and pans a' bangin' and Dossie shoutin'. We grinned at each other.

We went to work the next mornin'. I took my detour to the feed store. Jim went to the lumber company.

We stayed out in the barn at night and hid in the woods when Dossie come outside pretendin' she was searchin' for somethin'. We' knowed she was lookin' for us. The women didn't come back all week. Dossie was forced to take care of all the mooin', cluckin', barkin', moanin' animals without any help. Life wasn't so pretty for Dossie anymore. There was no one to boss around or work for her.

She'd stayed steady mad at the Creator for a long time. Me and Jim knowed it. We'd listened to her cuss Him out enough. Now the shoe was on the other foot. Seems like the Creator had stood enough of Dossie's Change. If the Creator hadn't got enough of it, me and Jim sure had.

On Friday night we set Dossie's groceries on the porch and sneaked out to my RV and got the hell out of there. We did it slow and purposeful the second weekend, but it was hard on us. We never seen hide nor hair of Dossie.

We come back Sunday evening.

Dossie was settin' in her rockin' chair on the front porch of the house again. She dropped her head and acted like she was readin' the book she held and didn't see or hear us. That action didn't fit anything we'd ever seen out of her.

Well, what's a son supposed to do when his Ma runs off her rocker? Take your Pa and get the hell out, I say.

Jim glanced at me. I could tell when we was in accord on this. Without a word, we did the least we had to right then to settle back in, then we silently headed past the barn and up on the trails as quick as we could. What we was doin' may have looked bad to somebody in the know about these matters, but we wasn't one of that crowd.

The fall days passed. Me and Jim winterized the barn and the RVs. We'd lived out winters before in them. No problem.

Dossie moved a couple of the women in with her and they built fires outside everywhere and chanted and danced around them while we hid out.

Me and Jim decided to take a long weekend off of work before snowfall. We took a few days off work and set extra groceries at Dossie's door on Friday night before we left. We drove both RVs to gauge how they'd do through the winter for us. They did fine. We bought extra anti-freeze and such to keep them in tip top shape.

We traveled up to King's Mountain, a place we liked, to gather the cookin' herbs we used. They come in this time of year. We went to old Barley's place and stayed with him a few days and picked sage and gathered other cookin' herbs. We trapped rabbits and squirrels and give them to old Barley. He'd need 'em for the winter. Then we headed home. The place looked deserted and quiet when we got there. Except there was a whole bunch of tire tracks in the dirt by the house. Was Dossie okay?

We went to the door of the house and knocked. Dossie screamed at us from inside. She called us varmints and much more. Including filthy names. We left and went to the barn. We looked at each other. Well, hell. It was still going on.

The next mornin', we went our separate ways to our jobs. The sheriff visited Jim at work first. Then he come to see me. He said for us to report to his office after work. He never mentioned what about. That was a very long, bad feelin' day for both of us.

We met up and went to the sheriff's office. He set us down in chairs and stood in front of us.

"Here's the bad news, boys. Your woman Dossie filed a missin' person's report on both of you."

Me and Jim looked at each other. Then we dropped our heads before he could see the wrath building up in our eyes.

To keep it down, my mind studied on the blue fairies I'd learned about from Dossie when I was young. The sheriff scolded us and told us not to leave again without telling Dossie. We thought at first, maybe the sheriff was joking, but no, he wasn't. I kept my mind elsewhere while he lectured us.

The blue fairies work with every kind of blue flower there is in existence. Other fairies work with other colors. But all fairies work with the colors of Nature, not anything else.

Blue fairies are shy and gentle, detail oriented, hard workers like me and Jim. They minded their own business, like me and Jim. They hurt from loud noises, like me and Jim. They helped each other like me and Jim had always helped Dossie.

They lived in devotion to each other, like me and Jim had lived our lives in devotion to Dossie.

Jim's voice interrupted my studies of the blue fairies. I listened to him tell the sheriff we wouldn't leave again without Dossie knowin' it. I heard the quiet outrage in his voice. So did the sheriff.

"We're all men here. We all know how it can get with women. Go on home."

He clapped Jim on the back and grinned.

**Goin' north to the mountains
where the snows last long and deep
Goin' up in the mountains
so I can unwind
lay my head down in peace
in a place unconfined.**

Part Nine

That night Jim and me walked for miles, neither of us sayin' a thing. But we were thinkin' the same thing. The next day, we went on about our business as usual.

Even though it went against our grain, we didn't buy animal feed or set groceries up against the door for Dossie on Friday night.

I watched Jim's Adams Apple workin'. He croaked out, "Let her get a damn job and take care of herself." His words come out like a sort of sob. I turned away. The blue fairies danced at the edge of my vision, soothing the fragments of devotion that were falling away. Interested, I noticed they were like pieces of hardened lotion, smooth and full of what once was.

The weekend come. We got ready to leave.

"Come on," I said. "Let's get them notes wrote."

We stuck one note on Dossie's door and dropped the other note off at the sheriff's office when we went through town. We slipped it under his door. It said Dossie Griggs had been notified that we were leavin' her place for a couple of days. We were both mortified. We was reportin' in like little school boys. It was devastating.

We spent the weekend right outside of town. We jist' couldn't go any further. We was afraid of what Dossie could do to us. She had trapped us. And we were both astounded and pissed off about it. At her for not carin' more about what she did to us. For not being more careful with our love for her. For the many, many mean things she had done to us for awhile now. The list was long. We'd forgiven all for a long time. Maybe too long. Now we didn't know if we could keep on doin' for her, though we knew we'd always care about her.

We sorted it out. We made a list.

Dossie had a home place now and seemed to like it.

She didn't want to travel any more.

But we did.

We'd endured stayin' there for her sake only.

We were not enamored of the animals.

Or her women friends.

Then we come down to the bottom line.

We didn't want to help Dossie anymore. Not after she called the cops on us when we hadn't done a damn thing wrong except escape from her mean craziness and irresponsibility for a little while.

Yep. Dossie had turned mean.

Dossie had turned on us.

We wanted to leave her there. She'd have to get a job. But she was good at that.

But if we left, she'd call the cops on us. Dossie had turned not only turned mean, she was making us mind. She would have us in prison before long. We both knew it. We'd die in there. Maybe that was her plan for us. We had to get away.

"I better go over a town or two aways' from here, where nobody knows Dossie or me, and find a lawyer and see what he says to do." Jim finally said.

I nodded. Neither of us could speak the word divorce. It had never once crossed our minds until Dossie penned us up with the sheriff.

It was a hard, lonely weekend, spent grievin' for who Dossie was before she went off her rocker.

We didn't trap, but we made a good fire to watch. We was told long ago that a good fire transforms negative energies into positive, useful energies. But we also knew that once a transformation starts, it will run its course, come hell or high water. We intended to live free.

Sometimes there is no goin' back. Dossie had alienated us with her spoilt ways while she was supposed to be transformin' into a Wise woman. She'd took up every meanness and crazy thing she could think of. We could never go back to the way it was before.

Well, it was over when we was threatened. Our very lives was in peril. She had threatened our very lives. Our innards. Our souls. The hurt run deep and blue as a river. The moon was never the same white above me again. I never asked Jim how it was for him.

We worked ever' day and set the groceries outside Dossie's door for her on Friday nights, like the sheriff ordered us to. We brought feed home for the animals, but we drew the line there. Dossie would have to see to them herself or get someone else to do it. We didn't think she could get us put in the pen for not feedin' her junk crew of varmints.

There was a phone booth in the back of the general store. We went in the store and I kept the owner busy so he couldn't eavesdrop on Jim and tell everybody in town. The man knew what I'd done after Jim slipped out of the telephone booth. He didn't like being tricked, but we bought a couple things, and he got better.

On Friday, we took off work early and Jim and me went to see the lawyer he'd called from the general store. His office was out on the end of a town about thirty miles away. It was in a little place that was well hid from people going by. Not in a goldfish bowl like up on Main Street in small town America. His office was small and surrounded by privacy fencing and trees. We parked about a mile away, then we hustled closer and slipped through the trees and tapped on the back door.

A young man opened the door and we stared at him.

He stared back. Then he said, "Come on in boys." he drawled. "I won't ask why you didn't come to the front door. This is a lawyer's office, after all."

He grinned. We looked him up and down. He was a young red head and a flashy dresser. That didn't bode well for us. We liked the color blue. People who liked blue and understood it, usually had fine brown hair. They paid attention to detail. He never even looked us over. People who favored the color blue owned voices that was mild and smooth instead of craggy and rough.

We turned to leave.

"The boss will be back in a minute."

We turned back around.

Just then, a middle aged man who looked like a beech owl came in the room. He had fine brown hair, blue eyes, and a regular voice with no bragging in it.

"My son," he indicated the young man. "He's just leaving."

"Good," Jim said.

An hour later and twenty bucks short, we left his office and sneaked away.

What he'd said was painful. Me and Jim hurt like son of a guns. He said during these days and times, the best we could do was for Jim to get a legal separation because we would have to accuse Dossie of something bad for legal grounds to divorce her. That way, we could still keep an eye on her or leave without the sheriff interfering as long as we left her a goodbye note.

Well, nothing was workin' out the way we planned. Dossie brought a new woman out to stay with her and they both started gettin' bold with us. The woman kept followin' us around with Dossie trailin' close behind her.

"Why aint ye' feedin' the animals?" the woman asked a bunch of times.

"Cat got ye' tongues?" she said. Well, we locked ourselves in the RV. The women laughed and went back to the house.

The next day after work, we drove over to the lawyer's office and started our legal separation from Dossie. The divorce could be got easy once the legal separation had been honored for a year, the lawyer said.

"You ready to leave that place boys? 'Cause that's what you'll have to do. You have to leave her."

We nodded. We was ready. The old Dossie was gone and the new Dossie was dangerous to every part of us. It was time to move on. Jim paid the money.

"The papers will be ready to sign in two weeks. That's because I have to file with the courts." the lawyer said.

"But we never married legal, so what's the need for court?" Jim asked.

The lawyer studied him. "That puts a new light on the matter."

"Set back down," he said. "We got some more talkin' to do."

We set down.

"This is goin' to be easier than you think because there's no common law marriage in this state. It doesn't recognize them. And she is domiciled here. And has been. Boys, let me shape this up for you. You're gonna' be free before long. And with you travelin' around like that all these years, I bet you never stayed in one state long enough to for the common law marriage to take effect."

"No, we never stayed anywhere very long." Jim answered.

Two weeks later, Jim signed papers givin' Dossie all the rights to the house and the property. The lawyer would hold them until we told him to give them to her. We didn't need to worry about a divorce.

Winter set in.

Back at home, Dossie started wanderin' around outside and settin' down in the snow.

"We gotta' git' outa' here before she takes sick, and I am blamed and put in the pen." Jim whispered to me.

We left as quick as we could. We never notified anybody that we was leavin' just in case they drummed up somethin' to take us to jail for.

We drove out of hell's parlor at 4:40 one Sunday mornin' real slow and easy, makin' the least amount of noise we could. We never looked back. We drove until we was too low on gas to go any further. We gassed up our RVs and hit the road again. Me and Jim talked on our two way radios to each other about gas and such. Nothing else. We talked when we stopped for the night, so nobody could hear us or report us.

The days turned into a week. We kept on goin' until we got clear to the other coast, a place we'd rarely been to. Dossie would be least likely to look for us there.

We let our hair and beards grow long until we didn't look like the same men any more. We found jobs that paid okay and kept them a little while, then moved on.

I quit studyin' on the blue fairies because it made me think about Dossie too much.

After awhile, I got a good job workin' up in the mountains at a nature park. Jim got hired on too. But I made the good money because of my forestry degree.

We settled into a cabin part way up the mountain. Nobody was around, and we went to work ever' day. We rested easy after awhile. A couple years went by, and we didn't need much. I saved up most of my money. I wasn't restless any more. We'd quit the road when we started hidin' out.

We bought some land up in Alaska and moved up there and built a cabin on it. I got a good job up there, too. Everything went into my name because of Jim's fear of Dossie findin' us and takin' everything again. We lived and thrived. We never saw Dossie again.

I finally went back to studyin' the blue fairies. I sent away for rare books on them. You know, the Elementals are very different up here in the north than they are down south. The blue fairies here are cold and withdrawn. They stay quiet and still except for the summer durin' which they are busy night and day savorin' flowers and breathin' deep of pollen.

The waters here are colder and darker blues. The sky is a rainbow and a stalker bringing sudden changes. It is not a steady blue with little sweet clouds like we knew before. Winters are long and that is good. We get by. Yep. We do.

Me and Jim put up with the Shadow for awhile. At first, we tried dancin' with it, trying to pacify it. We cooked for it, damned it, held it.

Everything we could think of to do, we did. It rushed out of left field and knocked us down. It stayed watchful, like a boxer, and took us down a peg or two every time it got a chance. It worked us over good, plenty of times. It became a rug puller and a greedy time user. It fed on our fear and dread.

This is what happened to us.

We couldn't fix it.
We couldn't repair it.
We couldn't help it.
So, we run away and made a new life for ourselves, me and Jim. We are landed hermits living in a northern cabin and our best spring and summer flowers are the blue Iris that require the winter sun to bloom. The Elementals that attend this species of flowers are devoted and true blue.

Me and Jim do the work and stay fit as we can and face each day pretty easy. We got the blue sky, the blue water lappin' at the cabin's beach front, and the blue flowers that bloom for the blue fairies. I've been here long enough now, that I've planted a whole field of 'em for them over these years.

Don't mistake it, though. Me and Jim still pack up our tents or RVs and go campin' whenever we want to. We go away and pick flowers and trap or fish.

We bathe in streams and send away for books on Nature. We're meat eaters and herb gatherers. We got us a boat, too.

www.ingramcontent.com/pod-product-compliance
Lightning Source LLC
LaVergne TN
LVHW041956060526
838200LV00002B/39